This book be...

JOOSH'S JUICE BAR
The Blue Banana Berry Adventure

Written by Josh Gottsegen

illustrated by Sehreen Shahzad

ISBN: 1493546848
ISBN-13: 978-1493546848
*
First Edition

Dedicated to NussyG

Welcome to Tropland Rainforest!

The most beautiful, colorful, absolutely wonderful rainforest in the world! Home to plants and animals from insects to mammals, trees and flowers with rain drop showers!

A wooden juice bar is built around the strongest tree
so even the smallest pair of eyes in the forest can see
that **Joosh's Juice Bar** is the best place to be!!

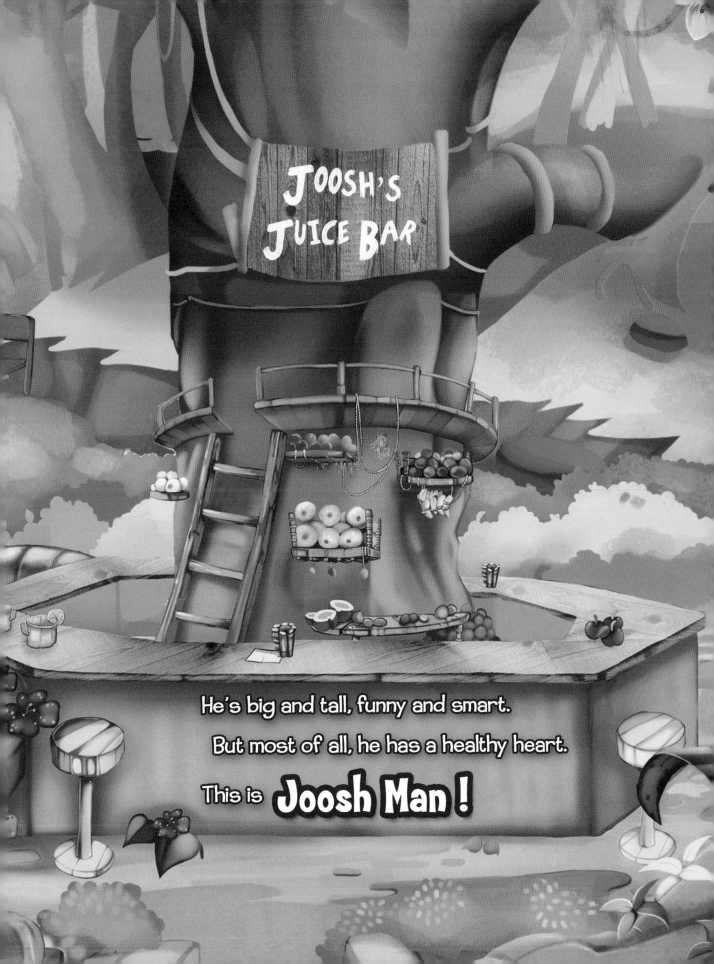

He's big and tall, funny and smart.

But most of all, he has a healthy heart.

This is **Joosh Man!**

"Heyo!"
Says Mo's friend, Randy.
He works at the juice bar
and is always so dandy.

Birds and bats,

kangaroos with hats,

monkeys and parrots,

bunnies with carrots,

butterflies and grasshoppers,

deer and moose

all lined up for

Joosh's fresh juice!

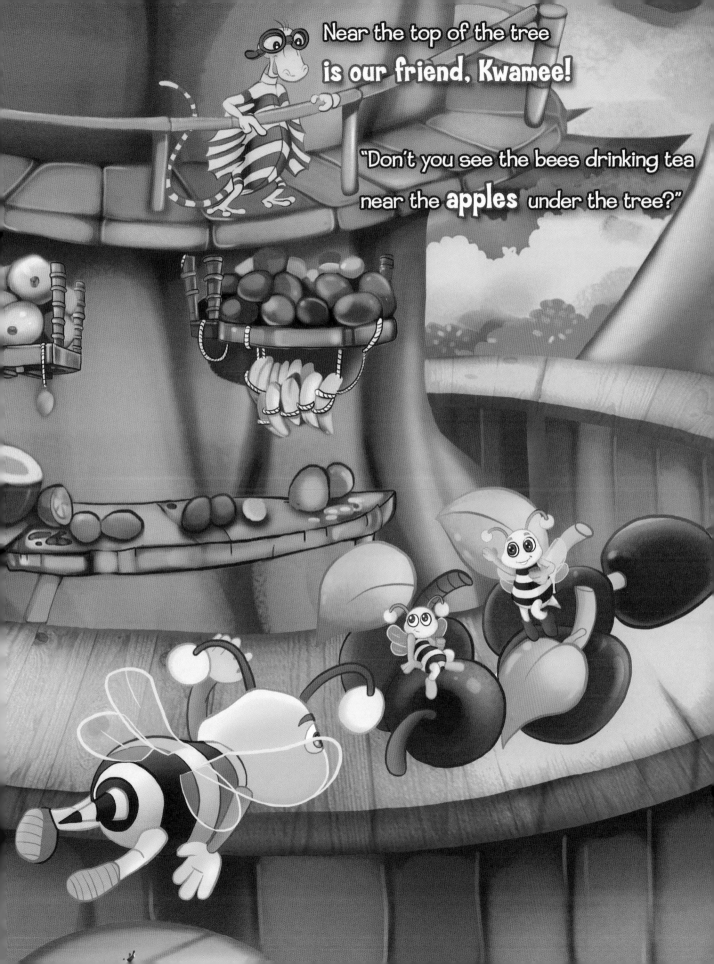

"There's no need for candy."

Says Joosh with a smirk.

"Fruit is a sweet treat,

now get back to work."

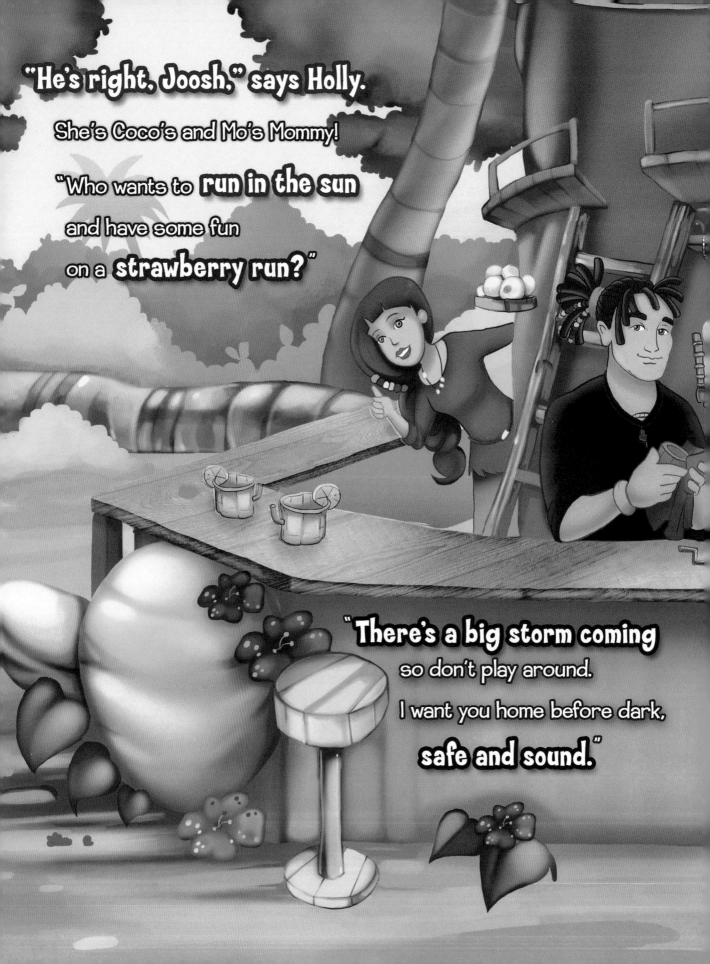

"He's right, Joosh," says Holly.

She's Coco's and Mo's Mommy!

"Who wants to **run in the sun**
and have some fun
on a **strawberry run?**"

"**There's a big storm coming**
so don't play around.
I want you home before dark,
safe and sound."

Ant-tack!

Holy centipedes!

They talked for a while without any objections,
until Paul got angry when Randy kept asking for directions.

They jumped through the trees
and ran through the fog
but now they are lost near the home of **Don Ribbit** the frog.

Don Ribbit the frog is
yellow and **blue.**
He lives in the swamps, he's mean and he's rude.

"Don't eat it! I have no doubt.
Can't you see the sign KEEP OUT?"

"Look at this fruit Coco! They have a shiny, blue glow!"

But **Coco** wouldn't eat them because they look like bad candy. In fact, she refused and would throw them at **Randy.**

When they came home there was no one around,
so they made a **new juice** with the berries they found.

"Where have you been, Mo? You were gone for so long.

Did you get the **strawberries?** Or is something wrong?"

"You were out near the swamps with the frogs and the fog?

Go see Doctor Boo, he'll know how to fix this blue."

"**Doctor Boo,** where are you?
Mo and Randy are glowing blue
and I just don't know what to do?"

"Hello, **Joosh.**
Hello, **Randy.**
Hello, **Mo** and **Coco.**

Oh sweet carrots, boys!
You have a **blue glow.**

To get to my office
you'll need to climb!
I have a flower for Coco,
it smells **lovely** and sublime."

"Hello Doctor Boo Boo!"

"**Doctor Boo** knows why you're blue.
You were up to no good
eating Don Ribbit's
junk food."

All the animals are now glowing blue after they drank the latest blue juice.

"Don Ribbit's berries are not ordinary.
He uses ingredients that are rotten and scary.
They may look tasty but keep this in mind,
don't eat anything you randomly find."

"Oh sweet carrots, it's about to **rain!**
Water is the cure and it's good
for your brain."

"Bye bye Boo Boo!"

"Just so you know, **Randy** and **Mo**, this is where our **strawberries** grow."

After it stopped raining
Mo was explaining
what took so long
to get home to his mom.

"I'm so happy to see you, it's true, it's true.
Best of all, **you're not glowing blue.**"

All the birds and bats, kangaroos with hats,

monkeys and parrots, bunnies with carrots,

butterflies and grasshoppers, deer and moose

stopped glowing blue from
the blue banana berry juice.

"We learned Don Ribbit's junk berries are no good for you.
So now we'll use **blueberries,**
a fruit that's supposed to be blue!"

The sun has set
and the **moon shines bright,**
now it's time to say
goodnight.

But **Randy** and **Mo**
were sad for being wrong.
They felt bad that everyone
glowed blue for so long.
Joosh tucked them in
and Holly sang them a song.

There are times in life that we make mistakes and are wrong,
**but always remember to stand tall and be strong.
Be nice and don't fight, eat healthy and right.**

Relax your eyes.

I love you.

Goodnight.

About the Author:

Josh Gottsegen is a Los Angeles native and strives to create a world where rhymes, optimism and healthy living inspire. Josh the "Joosh Man" has worked in the entertainment industry for years and wears many hats producing, writing, editing and designing creative projects. Instilled with the knowledge of eating healthy and treating people with respect at a young age by his family, Josh was motivated to create Joosh's Juice Bar to deliver positive entertainment with a healthy twist.

Feel free to email Josh directly,
jooshman@icloud.com

Made in the USA
San Bernardino, CA
11 December 2013